Bedtime Stories

For People of All Ages

KEN PIETRANIEC

PAGE PUBLISHING, INC.
Conneaut Lake, PA

First originally published by Page Publishing 2021

ISBN 978-1-6624-2264-5 (hc)
ISBN 978-1-6624-2263-8 (digital)

Printed in the United States of America

To my grandchildren and the joys of childhood
that keep the little kid in us alive and well.

Contents

Introduction..vii

Patience Is a Virtue..1

Being Kind Feels Good 13

Practice Makes Perfect 25

Jose' the Hugger 35

A Week at the Lake 49

Stella Gets Kittens 57

Growing Is Good 73

Introduction

These stories were written to help children learn important values to enrich their lives and make the world a better place to live. Some are designed to invite the listener to put themselves into the story. Though interaction is not required, it does encourage listener engagement.

Interacting with the story opens the door to empathy for the characters in the stories. The questions along the way invite the listener to respond and engage in the story. The mantra found in many of them conveys a value that all generations hope to pass on to the next. The vocabulary and review questions help provide additional access to understanding.

Patience Is a Virtue

tricycle—a bike with three wheels

disappointed—feeling sad when you don't get something that you wanted

patient—willing to wait for something that you want

virtue—something about you that makes you a better person

keeping your balance—not falling down

training wheels—extra wheels to help you keep your balance on a bicycle

confidence—believing that you can do something correctly (right)

compliment—something that somebody says about you that makes you feel good

practice—doing something over and over to help you do it correctly (right)

This was the day that Gracie had been waiting for. It was her birthday, and more than anything else, she hoped that she would get the new bicycle that she had wanted. Her tricycle was fun, but all her friends were now riding two-wheeled bikes. She couldn't keep up with them when they went riding together. Her legs were long enough to reach the pedals on her friends' bikes, and now she wanted one of her own.

When she came downstairs for breakfast, her parents were both there waiting for her with smiles on their faces. She saw her birthday cake on the kitchen table, and her parents started singing happy birthday to her.

After she blew out the candles, her mother told her that there was a big box in the living room with her name on it. She ran into the living room and started unwrapping the box that she hoped had a two-wheeled bike in it. Just as she thought, inside was the bike that she had been looking at in the store window for weeks. She had dreamed of getting it on her birthday, and now that dream came true.

She was so excited that she wanted to take it outside immediately and start riding it. Unfortunately, it had just started raining outside, so Gracie would have to wait until later to ride her new bike. She was disappointed. Her first day with her new bike did not go as planned.

Her mother saw that Gracie was disappointed. She told Gracie, "Sometimes we need to wait for something that we want. We waited nine months for you to be born. We didn't want to wait, but we had to be patient. We were patient because we knew that when you were born, we would be the happiest people in the world. That experience reminded us that *patience is a virtue.*"

Gracie asked her mom, "What is a virtue?"

Her mother told her, "A virtue is something about you that makes you a better person. Being kind is a virtue. Honesty is a virtue. And *patience is a virtue*."

That afternoon the rain stopped, and the sun came out. She could hardly wait to climb onto the seat and start riding her new bike. As she climbed up and grabbed the handlebars, her dad suggested that he hold onto the back of the seat as she started to pedal.

After a short distance, her dad asked if it was okay for him to let go of the seat. Full of confidence, Gracie said yes, and for a few seconds, she was riding the bike on her own. But suddenly, she lost her balance, and the bike didn't go where she wanted it to go. She fell and skinned her knee. The bike was okay, but Gracie was hurt. Sometimes falling down hurts. Gracie didn't understand how hard it can be to balance on a two-wheeled bike, but she wanted to try again. She remembered the saying "If at first you don't succeed, try, try again."

Her dad asked if she wanted to try it again, and she said yes. He held the bike as she climbed on, put her feet on the pedals, and grabbed the handlebars. He asked if she was ready, and she said yes. Just like before, he held the seat as she started to pedal. After a few seconds of pedaling and steering, he let go. And for a few more seconds, Gracie was riding her bike without her dad helping her. Then, like the time before, the bike wasn't doing what she wanted it to do, and she fell—again. She felt a little sad, but she wasn't ready to give up.

Her dad saw that she was disappointed, and he had an idea. He suggested training wheels. He told her that with training wheels, she would not fall over. They would help her keep her balance as she learned to ride her new bike. He also reminded her that she needed to be patient and that *patience is a virtue*.

Gracie was trying to be patient, and she really wanted to ride her new bike without her dad running behind her holding the seat. She agreed that maybe the best way to get what she wanted was to attach some training wheels to the back of the bike to avoid losing her balance and falling over.

The next day when her dad came home from work, he had the training wheels with him. She was excited to attach them to the bike so that she could ride it without falling down. Once they were on, she climbed onto the seat, and the bike didn't fall over. This made her happy. Then she grabbed the handlebars and started pedaling. Again, the bike didn't fall over, and she was moving ahead as her smiling dad got further and further behind her.

It worked! Gracie could ride her new bike without falling down. She knew that her dad was not holding the back of the seat.

When she leaned to her left side or her right side, the training wheels kept her from falling over. She was very happy.

After several weeks of riding her new bike and not falling down, Gracie asked her dad if she could try riding her bike without the training wheels. She was feeling very confident that she could keep her balance on the bike without falling over.

After two weeks of learning to balance her bike with the training wheels on, she was now feeling confident to try riding without them. Her dad agreed to let her try, but he reminded her to be patient.

They started out with her dad holding the seat behind her. But when he let go, she fell again. This made her sad and disappointed.

Her dad ran to see if she was hurt. No blood this time, only her feelings were hurt. Instead of crying, Gracie wanted to try again. She told her dad that she would be patient and not give up because she believed that *patience is a virtue*. Once again, Gracie got on her bike, her dad held the seat behind her, and she started pedaling. She believed that she could do it. And when her dad let go of the seat, she did it. She kept her balance and didn't fall.

Gracie was very happy, and her parents were also very happy. Not only did she learn to ride her bike without training wheels, but she also learned the value of being patient. By not giving up, she got what she wanted.

Gracie's dad reminded her that practice was an important part of her getting what she wanted.

Gracie's mom told her how proud she was that Gracie had the confidence to get up and try again after she fell down.

After hearing the compliments from her parents, she added that there was one other thing that helped her succeed. She told them that practice and confidence were important, but without patience, she might have just given up.

Being patient may not always be easy, but it can sometimes help you get something that you want very badly. Gracie learned that practice and confidence are important and that…

Patience is a virtue!

Review Questions

1. Who is the main character in the story?

2. In your own words, what is this story about?

3. What was your favorite part of the story?

4. Is there any part of the story that you did not understand?

Words to help you understand the stories

elder—an older person…not young

confused—not understanding something or someone

neighborhood—area around where you live

frown—a look of sadness…not happy

nest—where birds live

sweating—something your body sometimes does when it gets hot

organized—not messy

As Kenny was leaving the grocery store, he noticed a woman behind him with bags in both hands. After he walked through the door, he held it open for her, and a smile appeared on her face.

She said, "Thank you, young man. That was kind of you."

When he got home, he told his mother, "A lady called me kind today. I thought that the word *kind* meant 'what kind of apple do you like or what kind of dog do you have.'" Kenny was confused. *Have you ever felt confused?*

His mother told him that the word *kind* can also describe how you behave. When you are thoughtful and nice, you are being kind. When you treat someone badly, you are not being kind. She told him that being kind is a choice that some people make. You can choose to be kind.

Kenny took what his mother told him and went out to see if he could be kind again. He liked the way it made him feel the first time. He thought that maybe he could be kind in other ways than opening doors.

When he got outside, he saw his little sister trying to fly her kite. She was running with it behind her, but she couldn't get it off the ground. He could see that she was feeling unhappy and decided that there might be a way that he could help her.

He offered to hold it and run behind her until the kite flew up into the air. As soon as they started running together, he had to let go because the kite wanted to fly. The smile on his sister's face showed him, once again, that *being kind feels good*.

Kenny liked feeling good. As he walked away from his smiling sister, he was glad that he chose to help her.

After that, Kenny decided to walk down to the neighborhood park that had swings and a slide. After sliding down a couple of times, he decided to try the swings. He knew how much fun it was to swing high. He had no trouble going high on his swing, but he noticed that the boy next to him was having a hard time getting his started. He thought that this might be another chance for him to be kind.

Kenny got off his swing and gave the boy's swing a push. The frown on the boy's face turned into a smile that got bigger each time Kenny pushed the swing that went higher and higher. Kenny had found another way to be kind, and it felt good. When Kenny left the park, he could hear the boy yelling "Thank you!" from his smiling face.

As Kenny was walking on his way home from the park, he noticed something moving in the tall grass near him. When he got closer, he saw a baby bird that had fallen from its nest in the tree. He felt that the baby bird needed some help.

Do you remember a time when you needed some help?

He wasn't sure what to do, but knew that with all the cats and dogs in the neighborhood, a bird that couldn't fly wouldn't last long lying there on the ground. He knew that he needed to do something to help the baby bird.

He bent over and gently lifted the baby bird and put it back in its nest. The bird was chirping and seemed to be glad to be back in its home. As he let go of the baby bird, he realized that you can be kind to things other than people, and once again thought to himself, *Being kind feels good.*

When Kenny got home, he saw his father cutting the lawn. It was very hot that day, and he noticed that his father was sweating a lot. He was too young to offer help cutting the lawn, but he wanted to find a way to be kind to his father.

So Kenny went into the house and came out with a large glass of cold water. When his dad saw Kenny with the glass of water, a big smile appeared on his face. His dad was glad to take a short break to rest.

"Thank you very much," his dad said. "That was very thoughtful of you. You didn't have to do that, but I sure am glad that you did."

It was at that moment that Kenny truly understood what it meant to be kind. Being kind is something you do not because you *have to* but because you *want to,* and we know that *being kind feels good.*

After dinner, Kenny wanted to find a way to be kind to his mother. As she was clearing the table, Kenny decided to help her. He wasn't expected to help clean the kitchen after dinner, but he noticed a smile on his mother's face when he carried the dirty dishes to the sink. As she loaded the dishwasher, Kenny grabbed a washcloth and wiped off the dinner table. It wasn't the same as saving a bird's life, but it made him feel just as good.

With homework to do, Kenny went to his room with a smile on his face. After he finished his homework, he noticed that his backpack was full of old papers, candy wrappers, broken pencils, and many other things that just got in the way when he was looking for something that he needed. He thought how nice it would be to have his backpack clean and organized like it was on the first day of school.

He decided to dump it out on his bed and get rid of all the things that he didn't need. He saved the good pencils, put the loose papers into his notebook, and dumped out the cookie crumbs. He was amazed at all the extra room he had in the pack after he put everything back in. By cleaning out and organizing his backpack, he was being kind to himself—and it made him feel good,

As he crawled into bed, he thought about all the kind things he had done that day and how they all made him feel good. Kenny really liked that being kind not only made him feel good, but being kind also helped others feel good—maybe even happy. After he turned off the light, Kenny fell asleep dreaming of ways that he could be kind tomorrow, because he now knew for sure that *being kind feels good*.

Review Questions

1. Who is the main character in the story?

2. In your own words, what is this story about?

3. What was your favorite part of the story?

4. Is there any part of the story that you did not understand?

Practice Makes Perfect

Words to help you understand the stories

practice—doing something over and over again to get it right

disappointed—feeling sad when you hoped to feel good

talent show—a time when people can perform in front of others

confident—feeling positive that you can do something

nervous—feeling unsure that you can do something

applauding—people clapping their hands together

proud—feeling very good after doing something

Nora had been playing the piano for two years. She was no longer a beginner and wanted to play a song in the talent show at her school. Many of her friends were entering. Some danced, some sang, and some played other musical instruments, but none of her friends played the piano.

Can you name other musical instruments?

Nora's mother thought that being in the talent show was a good idea. Together, they picked out a song for Nora to play. The only problem was that it was not an easy song, and sometimes Nora would make a mistake when playing it.

She didn't make the mistake every time, but she could never be sure that it would be perfect when she played it. Her mother suggested that she practice it over and over until the mistake disappeared, because her mother believed that *practice makes perfect*.

Her mother said, "I know that you are tired of practicing, but maybe a couple of extra minutes will help you get what you want. You still have a few days to practice, and the rest of the song sounds perfect."

Nora practiced an extra ten minutes, but she still made the same mistake almost every time she tried to play the song. She felt disappointed.

Have you ever felt disappointed?

When Nora's mother came back into the room, she saw that Nora felt sad because she kept making the same mistake. She thought about giving up and not playing in the talent show.

"I'll never get it right," she told her mother. "Maybe I should just forget the whole thing. Who cares if I don't play in some stupid old talent show." She really thought about giving up.

Can you remember a time when you just wanted to give up on something?

Seeing that Nora was upset, her mother tried to comfort her. "No one is making you play in the talent show. If you want to quit, you can. But you still have one more day to decide, and maybe one more day of practice will make the difference."

Nora got up early the day of the talent show to practice one last time. She was very pleased that each time she played the song, she didn't make the mistake. This made her happy and confident. She went to school that day believing that she could play the song perfectly.

Nora couldn't wait to get to school and play her song in the talent show. She thought about all the hours of practice that she had put into getting ready for it. She understood what her mother meant when she said that *practice makes perfect.*

As she waited for her turn to play, Nora didn't feel nervous at all like she thought she would. Instead, she felt confident. Nora was glad that she decided to practice the extra hours.

Can you remember a time when you felt nervous or confident?

When her name was called, Nora walked out onto the stage, sat down at the piano, and started playing the song. She didn't even think about making the mistake that disappeared with her extra practice. It was perfect. She played the whole song without a single mistake.

When she finished the song, a huge smile appeared on her face. She felt very happy. The audience was applauding, and she could see from the looks on her parents' faces that they felt as happy as she did. She also felt proud.

Have you ever felt proud of something you did?

School was over after the talent show. Then, they all rode home in the car. Her mother was still smiling when she said that she also was proud of her daughter. She knew that Nora could have given up, but she didn't.

Nora's dad was still smiling too. He told her that he always believed that she could do it. He knew how much she practiced and how patient she needed to be.

And we all know that Nora was still smiling. She was glad she decided to play in the talent show. She was glad that she decided to practice those extra hours. Most of all, she was glad to learn that *practice makes perfect!*

Review Questions

1. Who is the main character in the story?

2. In your own words, what is this story about?

3. What was your favorite part of the story?

4. Is there any part of the story that you did not understand?

34

Jose' the Hugger

This is a story about a boy who learned early in life the values of hugging and the different kinds of hugs. From his early childhood, through his growing up, to his becoming a parent and a grandparent, Jose' was always proud to be a hugger.

A grandmother's hug

Jose' first learned how good a hug can feel when he was a very young child. In addition to the hugs he received from his parents, he never forgot how wonderful a hug felt from his grandmother. She was a big woman, and he was just a little boy. With her arms around him, she would lift him up and hold him so close that he felt that he was a part of her body. A full-body hug from a grandmother is something that you always remember.

A brother's and sister's hug

Jose' loved his brother and his sister. When he was growing up, they often played together even though they weren't the same age. Hugging was something that they all learned to do as children. Morning, noon, or night, their hugging always reminded them of the special relationship that they had then and would share for the rest of their lives.

A friend's hug

When Jose' started school, he had many friends. He didn't hug them as much as he hugged his family, but he learned that a hug could do more than just let a person know that you loved them. A hug could let someone know that you were sorry. A hug could help make a new person feel welcomed. A hug could help you feel brave. A hug could help Jose' feel better when he fell down and got hurt.

Giving and receiving a hug

As Jose' got older, he realized that hugging was a special way for him to express himself. He always enjoyed hugging his family and good friends, but he learned that hugging wasn't something that you could do with everyone. Receiving a hug is something the person needs to be ready for; otherwise, it is just a one-way hug—not nearly as satisfying as a two-way hug.

A goodbye hug

Once during summer vacation, Jose' went to visit his cousin who lived in another state. It was his first trip on an airplane and the first time he would be away from his family for more than one day. When it was time for him to board the plane, he felt a tear in his eye. He wasn't sure what caused it, but he felt a little scared of getting on the plane and leaving his parents behind. The goodbye hugs he got from his mom and dad before boarding the plane were different than the ones he got at home. They lasted a little longer, and he found himself thinking of how much he loved his parents.

A sad hug

One year when it was time for Jose' to go back home from summer camp, he discovered that a hug doesn't always make you feel happy. The goodbye hugs he gave to all the people he met at camp felt a little sad to him. He made many new friends and had many wonderful stories to share when he returned home. But he also realized that he might never see his new friends ever again. They were all going home, and summer camp would soon become just a memory. It was the first time that he felt sad while hugging.

A sadder hug

When he got home from camp, his parents took him to the hospital to visit his grandmother. She had a heart attack while he was gone, and they were afraid that she was going to die. When they got up to her room, he noticed that there were many machines helping to keep her alive. She woke up for a few minutes after he got there, and she greeted him with a warm smile. As she always did, she opened her arms for a hug. This hug was different that any hug he had ever gotten from her. Her weakness made him do most of the hugging. And there was that tear again, as he realized that it might be the last hug he ever got from her.

Other kinds of hugs

As Jose' grew toward adulthood, he shared many hugs with many, different people. There were the teammate hugs after their soccer victories. There were the high school hugs at graduation. And of course, there were all the family hugs at birthdays, weddings, and funerals. Jose's ability to hug was something that he thought everybody had. Who wouldn't want to hug?

43

Not for everyone

The fact is that not everybody is a hugger. Not every child is raised with the pleasure of feeling hugged when they are young. Some parents aren't huggers. Some grandparents aren't huggers. Some brothers and sisters aren't huggers. There are many different reasons that some people hug more than others while some don't hug at all. Jose' understood this, but he felt a little sorry for the nonhuggers. He knew from a lifetime of experience that hugs could make you feel happy, hugs could help you feel brave, and that hugs could make you feel loved.

Adult hugs

Eventually, Jose' grew up and got married. His wife was a hugger, and so were their kids. Jose' got to feel the special hug of a wife. He also got to feel that special love you feel when you are hugging a child that you brought into the world. It is a feeling that is hard to put into words. Hugging his parents when he was young always felt different from all the other hugs he gave and received. Now, as a parent, he understood the special kind of love that his parents felt when they hugged him as a child.

Grandparent hugs

When Jose's children grew up, they also got married and had children of their own. As a grandparent, he had a special kind of relationship with all of them. He loved spending time with each one. He enjoyed playing with them. He enjoyed helping them learn to read and write. He even enjoyed practicing their multiplication tables with them. He actually helped them learn many things. But there was something that his grandchildren helped him to learn— something he could only learn from them.

Jose's grandchildren helped him learn how good the hug from a grandchild can feel. Without his grandchildren, Jose' would have never been able to feel that kind of joy that his grandmother obviously felt when she hugged him as a little child. His lifetime of being a hugger helped him understand that sharing a hug can be one of the best feelings in the world.

Review Questions

1. Who is the main character in the story?

2. In your own words, what is this story about?

3. What was your favorite part of the story?

4. Is there any part of the story that you did not understand?

A Week at the Lake

The plan was to spend a week in a cabin at a lake with my cousins, aunts, and uncles. All the families scheduled their summer vacation for the same time so we could all share the week at the lake together. After weeks of planning, the day came for us to pack for the trip. Mom pretty much told us what clothes to bring, but we got to decide on other things like books and toys to help us enjoy the week at the lake.

When we arrived in the late afternoon, I wanted to run down to the beach, but Dad wanted us to help unload the car. The trunk was jam-packed with suitcases and boxes. Dad carried the heavy stuff, but there were plenty of lighter things to carry in. Mom asked if anyone was hungry, but my desire to get my feet wet blocked out any hunger that I may have felt.

The sun was shining, and the sand was soft. I was so excited to finally be there that I went in the water as far as I could without getting my clothes wet. The drop-off was gradual, and there was plenty of water and shoreline to explore. The other families arrived earlier, so my cousins came out when they saw me. We all shared the excitement of being there.

That evening, we built a campfire on the beach. We collected plenty of firewood and built it far away from the front cottage. All the adults brought a folding chair to sit on, but most of us kids just sat in the sand. The conversations and laughter went on for hours as we all caught up on one another's news. All us kids made smores and had fun trying to cook the perfect marshmallow.

The next morning, the sun was shining when I got up. After a bowl of cereal, I headed right for the beach. After blowing up my air mattress, I set sail for the sandbar. My cousins told me that they discovered a shallow area of water far out past the deeper water. When I got out there, the color of the water changed, and I could actually see the shallow sandy bottom. When I slid off my air mattress, I found myself standing in knee-deep water, but I could still see and hear people on the beach.

As the days rolled by, much time was spent swimming, floating on the air mattress, playing with my cousins, and exploring the area. The beach to the left and right went on for far as I could see. I enjoyed walking along the shoreline and in the nearby woods. Mom always wanted to know where I was going but knew that we were in a safe area and trusted me to be careful.

Tuesday morning, we got up early to go fishing. Along with three of my cousins, three uncles, and two aunts, we loaded our fishing gear into the cars and drove to the boat dock in town. My uncles arranged for us to go out on what they called a charter boat. A charter boat holds a lot of people who want to fish from a boat but don't have a boat of their own. Once we got on board, we found a place where we could all sit together. Fishing from shore is fun, but fishing out on a boat is even more fun.

The hours passed quickly, and at noon, it was time to head back to land. After getting off the boat, we drove back to the cabins and unloaded our gear. We told all our fishing stories to those who didn't go with us and watched as my aunts and uncles cleaned the fish so we could eat them. Dinner that evening was all-you-can-eat fish and chips. Even after everyone finished eating, there was still plenty of fish leftover. Now I know how good fresh fish can taste.

On Wednesday, after dinner and another fun day at the beach, my parents took our family for a drive into town. The cabins at the lake were about five miles from any stores, and my mom needed a few things to get through the rest of the week. So after dinner, we all got into the car for an evening adventure.

After we were through food shopping, we took a walk along the main street of town. There were plenty of souvenir shops and stores. In one of them, I saw some diving masks. I thought how fun it would be to be able to see underwater while I was swimming. Having a mask to wear while swimming this week sounded like a good idea to me. I asked my parents if I could get it and got really excited when they said yes. I tried on several masks and finally found the one that I liked most.

After leaving the store with my best souvenir of the week, Dad suggested that we take a walk on the long pier at the state park in town. On our way there, we stopped and got ice-cream cones to eat along the way. At the pier, there was plenty to see. A lot of people had boats tied up to the docks. On the shore, there were people swimming; and as we walked the pier, we saw many people fishing. When we got to the end of the pier, the sun was going down, and it was starting to get dark. We watched as the sky turned colors from blue to purple to bright pink. It was a wonderful way to end another wonderful day.

Thursday was game night. Everyone was either inside or outside the larger cottage where my aunts, uncles, and cousins were staying. The adults were playing card games, and all us kids were playing different board games that we brought. Along with the Game of Life that I brought, there was Yahtzee, chess and checkers, Connect Four, Battleship, and Monopoly. It was fun staying up later than usual playing different games with all of my cousins.

After sleeping in Friday morning, my uncle Louie led all of us kids on a nature hike. We headed down the beach and soon found a path into the woods. After a few minutes, we saw our first deer. There was a doe and a fawn out in the clearing having breakfast. We all paused and kept still and quiet as the two deer watched us watching them.

Further down the path when I was walking by myself, I had a scary experience. Suddenly out of nowhere, a snake slithered by me so close that I almost stepped on it. When a little scream jumped out of my mouth, everyone came running. The snake had disappeared by the time they got there, and my uncle told us that it was probably just a garter snake, one that couldn't hurt us. Before we finished our nature hike, we saw an eagle, rabbits, chipmunks, seagulls, and baby frogs.

Saturday was the last full day of our vacation. After spending most of the day on the beach and in the water, we had a barbecue and our last campfire. As it got dark, people started sharing their favorite memory of the week that was now behind us. For my brother Ricky, it was catching his first fish. For my other brother Eddie, it was the nightly campfires. For my sister Mary Anne, it was learning how to swim.

When it came my turn, I had a few memories to pick from but decided that my daily trips out to the sandbar topped my list. Being out there by myself, far away from shore just floating on my air mattress, became my "happy place" that week. It was a memory and a feeling that I would take home with me. Now I know what Mom and Dad mean by having a happy place.

Sunday morning, everyone gathered at the front cottage for a celebration breakfast. The sun was shining, and everyone was happy. Visiting my relatives at home was always nice, but having everyone together at the same time for a full week was a new experience. When it was time to say goodbye, there was lots of hugging going on. After spending the week together playing, eating, swimming, staying up late, and having loads of fun every day, I felt a little sad that it was going to end.

And then, just before we headed back to our cottage to finish packing and load up the car for our trip home, my uncle Louie said that he had an announcement to make. During the adult card games Thursday night, the adults decided that the week went so well that we all should plan on doing it again next year. All of us kids let out a loud cheer, knowing that we had more fun to look forward to next summer.

Review Questions

1. Who is the main character in the story?

2. In your own words, what is this story about?

3. What was your favorite part of the story?

4. Is there any part of the story that you did not understand?

Stella Gets Kittens

When Stella and her dad moved in with her grampa, they brought along Pip, their cat. Like most ten-year-olds, Stella loved her cat. Pip was a fun playmate and loved to sleep with Stella. He purred when she read to him and greeted her at the door whenever she got home. Pip was the next best thing to having a brother or sister.

The move was not easy for Stella or Pip. They had to leave their neighborhood and their friends who lived there. And even though there were new friends to be made, Stella could tell that Pip was having a hard time adjusting. When he went outside, he stayed out longer than he did at their other home.

And then one night it happened. Pip didn't come home. Stella's dad told her to wait until the next morning when he was sure that Pip would come home after a night out. He told her that cats do that sometimes. She wanted to believe him and did her best to fall asleep without him that night.

The next morning, Stella got up early hoping to find Pip sleeping somewhere in the house. She searched every room calling out to him. After going into every room twice, she decided to try outside. Still no Pip.

Her dad offered to help look for Pip and told her that they could post a Lost Cat sign in the neighborhood, hoping that one of their neighbors might have seen him.

After two weeks, still no Pip. Since this made Stella very sad, her dad suggested that maybe they should think about getting another cat. Stella didn't want to believe that Pip was never coming back, but the thought of getting another cat made her feel a little bit better.

As they looked around places to get another cat, Stella's grampa saw an ad in the newspaper for kittens. When he suggested to Stella that they get a kitten, her eyes lit up. She remembered how much fun she had with Pip when he was a kitten. She knew that no cat could ever take the place of Pip, but the thought of having a new kitten to play with excited her.

Grampa showed Stella and her dad the ad he saw in the pet section of the newspaper:

> Kittens looking for a home: We have 4 adorable kittens ready for adoption.
>
> They are 8 weeks old, cat litter trained, and ready to move to a new home.
>
> Call Teresa at 562-8681.

Stella wanted to call right away. Her dad called, and the woman who answered told him that yes, the kittens were still available. After getting the address, Stella and her dad drove to the woman's house.

When they got there, they knocked on the door and were greeted by the owner of the kittens. As they entered, they became aware of a house filled with cats. There were cats everywhere. When they asked about the kittens, they were led into a room where the kittens were hanging out. The four kittens were busy playing, but when Stella and her dad entered the room, two of them looked up. They left their playmates and approached Stella.

She bent over to pet them, and they immediately started purring. Stella knew that they came just looking for one kitten but asked her dad if they could take both of them home. Seeing how happy the thought of bringing them home made Stella, her dad couldn't resist. They told the woman that they wanted both kittens. As happy as Stella was to think about taking a kitten home with her, now she was twice as happy.

Adjusting to their new home

It didn't take long for the kittens to adjust to their new home. They were already trained to use the cat litter box, but Grampa didn't want to take any chances of "an accident" the first few days, so they spent their first week in the kitchen and dining room with the doors closed. They had everything that they needed, including a cat condo. Having new toys and each other to play with, their first week in their new home went well for everyone. Since they showed that they would use the litter box, Grampa decided that it would be okay for them to explore the other rooms of the house.

The second week, the door to the family room opened for them. Their two-room world turned into a three-room world. The family room not only had carpeting, but it also provided a very large area for them to run around and explore. Again, everything in that room was new to them. They now had fish in an aquarium to look at, a door to the outside to look through, and a couch and recliner to climb on. They still went back to their original two-room world to eat, use the litter box, and sleep, but they now had a whole bunch of new places to play and lie down and take their naps.

The sleepover

One weekend, Stella scheduled a sleepover with two of her best friends. She knew how much fun kittens were and wanted to share the fun with her friends. The kittens were nonstop entertainment. They all stayed up very late that night, and everyone had a good time.

The next morning the kittens were the first ones up. With all the girls still sleeping, the kittens didn't hesitate to climb all over them and their sleeping bags. They even crawled inside a couple of times. The kittens enjoyed playing with the girls as much as the girls enjoyed playing with them.

Going outside

The time came for the kittens to explore beyond the inside of the house. They totally enjoyed their first weeks inside, climbing, hiding, and running all over the place. One of their more frequent stops between playing was looking out the windows. They saw another whole world on the other side of the glass doors. They were satisfied with their indoor life but seemed eager to discover and explore what it was like outside.

They were happy the day when the door to the outside was finally opened for them. They naturally were very timid and shy about stepping outdoors but soon discovered that it was safe enough to go out and start sniffing things. They sniffed everything. That's what kittens do when everything is new to them. They discovered a bigger world of sights, sound, and smells.

Among their discoveries were birds above them, soft grass below them, and bees pollinating the raspberry patch around them. The raspberry bushes were so thick they provided a kind of raspberry forest that the kittens could run into to play, hide, or do whatever else they felt like doing. After a few days of visiting the outside for a few hours, they started hanging out at the outside door every morning, waiting for it to open so they could go out.

It would not be long before the kittens would discover a way to get out of the yard, but for the time being, they had more than enough to keep them happy. Every day was a new adventure. They enjoyed chasing the flies, found many places to take their naps, and got used to using the cat door whenever they wanted to go outside.

Stella occasionally thought of Pip and still missed him, but living with the kittens helped her get used to the fact that Pip wasn't around anymore. She would never stop loving Pip, but now she had two cats to love—and two cats to love her.

On the other side of the fence

The day came when the kittens discovered that climbing the cherry tree could get them to the top of the six-foot fence. Once up there, the wide surface and their perfect balance allowed them to walk the perimeter of the fenced-in yard. On the other side of one fence was a dog. At first, they were frightened. As time went on, they all became friends.

But on a different side of the fence, there were two large barking dogs. Of these two dogs, the cats were terrified. They stopped walking that section of the fence and used the cherry tree to explore life outside of their yard.

Outside the yard was a whole different world. Without fences, they had the freedom to explore as far as they could see. It didn't take long for them to become part of the neighborhood and recognized as permanent residents. Stella knew that she lived in a safe neighborhood and trusted that the cats would always find their way home.

Well, one evening, they didn't. It had been dark for hours, and it was getting close to Stella's bedtime. They didn't come home at dinnertime like they usually did.

Stella decided to take a walk through the neighborhood, hoping to find them. As she walked, she called their names over and over until she arrived back home.

She arrived home without the cats, and since it was past her bedtime, she went right to bed. When she closed her eyes, she thought of Pip. She remembered how sad she was when he didn't come home. She remembered sleeping by herself those nights with no cat to cuddle with. She fell asleep hoping and believing that the two cats would come home before morning.

The next morning when she awoke, she discovered two kittens sleeping by her side. As the cats woke up, Stella started petting both of them at the same time, and they started purring. They were as happy to be home with Stella as she happy to be home with them.

Review Questions

1. Who is the main character in the story?

2. In your own words, what is this story about?

3. What was your favorite part of the story?

4. Is there any part of the story that you did not understand?

Growing Is Good

Words to help you understand the story

Soil is earth where plants can grow.

If you are **afraid**, you feel scared.

If you feel **confused**, you do not know what to do because you do not understand what is going on.

A **conversation** is talk between two or more people.

If you **trust** someone, you believe that they are honest and will not hurt you.

You feel **relieved** after you stop worrying about something

74

A flowerpot, like a house and a pair of shoes, provides a place to grow. We grow while living in a house, a flower grows while living in a pot, and our feet grow living much of their time in our shoes. We need a place to grow—and get bigger.

As time goes on, our shoes get too small for our feet. The truth is that our shoes don't get smaller, but our feet get larger. This is called growing, and *growing is good.*

Have you ever planted a seed and watched the plant grow? It starts very small, and if it is taken care of, it grows. If it is not taken care of, it does not grow—it doesn't get large, and soon it will die.

This is not a story about a person. It is a story about a plant named Petunia. It is a story about living and growing—and *growing is good.*

Like all of us, Petunia started out small. She lived in a very pretty flowerpot on a shelf with many other happy and healthy plants. She liked her home. She liked her friends. She was very happy.

Have you ever felt happy?

One day, Petunia saw that her roots were coming up out of the soil around her. She knew that her roots were supposed to stay in the soil to take in the food and water to keep her alive—and help her grow—because we all know that *growing is good*!

Each day Petunia saw more and more of her roots coming up out of the soil. And each day as more roots appeared, she felt weaker and her branches started sagging. Some leaves even started falling off. This made Petunia sad.

Have you ever felt sad?

Petunia did not know why her branches were sagging or why her leaves were falling off. She felt weaker than she had ever felt before. She wondered if she was dying. Not only was she feeling sad, she was now feeling afraid.

Have you ever felt afraid?

Then one day, she heard the conversation of the people who lived in the house. These were the people who fed her and watered her and kept her healthy and alive.

One of them said, "Petunia is not looking well. Does she need more light? Does she need more water?"

The other person said, "I think that she has outgrown her flowerpot. Maybe we need to give her a bigger pot and more room to grow."

Petunia had no idea of what they were talking about. A bigger flowerpot? More room to grow? What was wrong with the pot she was in—the one she had grown up in? Why would they want to take her out of a place where she felt happy?

She was sad that her leaves were falling off. She liked the life on her shelf with her friends. She wondered why the people who took care of her would want to change the place where she lived? Petunia was confused.

Have you ever felt confused?

The people carried her to a room outside of the house. This room had a very large pile of dirt. It also had many beautiful flowerpots that were empty. She had never seen empty flowerpots. All of the flowerpots that she had seen always had a flower or a plant in them.

One of the people picked her up and gently lifted her out of her flowerpot—her home for as long as she could remember. She had no idea what was happening. They had always taken good care of her. They always gave her what she needed. She had to believe that they were doing something that needed to be done. Petunia trusted them.

Do you have someone that you trust? More than one person?

What they were doing was taking her from the pot she had lived in and moving her to a larger flower pot—one that had more room, one that would allow her roots to stay below the soil like they were supposed to, one that would allow her to grow, because as we know *growing is good*!

Petunia liked her new home—a beautiful flowerpot that was a little larger than the one she was in before. All of her roots were below the soil, like they were supposed to be. And she noticed that her leaves were no longer sagging or looking like they were dying.

After the people were through planting her in the larger flowerpot, she was taken back to the shelf with her friends. She was glad to see them, and they were glad to see her happy and healthy in her new flowerpot.

As the days passed, she grew healthier and stronger. Instead of sagging branches, she noticed that she was growing new leaves—and some of the leaves had flowers growing on them. She had never been so big or so strong or so happy. By putting her into a larger flowerpot, the people had not only kept her alive, but they had given her a chance to grow, and we know that *growing is good*!

This story of Petunia, the potted plant, has a happy ending because the people who took care of Petunia knew that for her to be the biggest and best plant that she could be, she needed a new home—a larger flowerpot to grow in. If she had stayed in the smaller pot that she was born in, she might have never turned into the large, healthy, beautiful plant that she was now.

So what did Petunia learn from her experience? One of the things she learned is that to be the best plant that she could be, she needed to trust the people who loved her. She needed to believe that they knew what was best for her.

Sometimes, people also need to trust others and change the place where they are growing. To be the best, happiest, and healthiest person that we can be, we need to be sure that the place we are living is helping us grow, because everyone knows that *growing is good*!

Review Questions

1. Who is the main character in the story?

2. In your own words, what is this story about?

3. What was your favorite part of the story?

4. Is there any part of the story that you did not understand?

About the Author

Ken's thirty years in public education provided ample opportunity for him to spend time with and understand children. After he successfully raised four of his own, his retirement found him traveling, painting, gardening, and writing. Journaling since his college days, he decided to take on the project of writing a book.

His résumé referred to him as a "middle school junkie." Besides a bounty of successful years in the classroom, he also served as a counselor, intervention specialist, assistant principal, dean of students, teacher coach, and finished off his thirty years as a school librarian. His love for children went far beyond the classroom and his home. A loving relationship with his grandchildren planted the seeds for this book.

CPSIA information can be obtained
at www.ICGtesting.com
Printed in the USA
LVHW052046210521
688197LV00002B/16